Where Are You Going, Baby Lincoln?

Books for early readers
FROM KATE DiCAMILLO AND CHRIS VAN DUSEN

Mercy Watson
Mercy Watson to the Rescue
Mercy Watson Goes for a Ride
Mercy Watson Fights Crime
Mercy Watson: Princess in Disguise
Mercy Watson Thinks Like a Pig
Mercy Watson: Something Wonky This Way Comes

Tales from Deckawoo Drive
Leroy Ninker Saddles Up
Francine Poulet Meets the Ghost Raccoon
Where Are You Going, Baby Lincoln?
Eugenia Lincoln and the Unexpected Package

Volume Three

Where Are You Going, Baby Lincoln?

Kate DiCamillo

illustrated by Chris Van Dusen

CANDLEWICK PRESS

Text copyright © 2016 by Kate DiCamillo
Illustrations copyright © 2016 by Chris Van Dusen

First paperback edition 2017

Library of Congress Catalog Card Number 2016940244
ISBN 978-0-7636-7311-6 (hardcover)
ISBN 978-0-7636-9758-7 (paperback)

18 19 20 21 22 BVG 10 9 8 7 6 5 4

Printed in Berryville, VA, U.S.A.

This book was typeset in Mrs. Eaves.
The illustrations were done in gouache.

Candlewick Press
99 Dover Street
Somerville, Massachusetts 02144

visit us at www.candlewick.com

For Holly
K. D.

For Cricket and Dylan, who went west
C. V.

Chapter One

Baby Lincoln was dreaming.

In the dream, she was sitting on a train. Her hands were folded in her lap. The seat beside her was empty. Baby turned her head and looked out the window and saw that the dark sky was filled with stars, hundreds of them, thousands of them.

The train was going very fast, and the stars were falling through the sky, one after the other, chasing each other, leaving behind them great trails of light.

"Oh," said Baby, "shooting stars."

The train rushed through the starry darkness and Baby was entirely happy. *I wonder where I am headed,* she thought. *I cannot wait to find out. I am on a necessary journey.*

"Baby!" someone shouted. "You must wake up immediately!"

Baby woke up.

Her sister, Eugenia, was standing over her.

Eugenia had her hands on her hips.

"It is late, Baby. It is time to get on with our day," said Eugenia. "Goals must be set. Lists must be made. Tasks must be accomplished."

"Yes, Sister," said Baby.

At the breakfast table, Eugenia had Baby write down the day's goals.

Eugenia was very fond of goals.

"Goal number one," said Eugenia. She cleared her throat. "The mouse problem must be dealt with. We are on the verge of an infestation. You, Baby, will go to Clyde's Bait, Feed, Tackle, and Animal Necessities and purchase mousetraps."

"But mousetraps kill mice," said Baby.

"Exactly," said Eugenia.

"Oh, Sister," said Baby.

"Do not 'Oh, Sister' me. You are too soft for this world, Baby. You must be firm and resolute, particularly with mice. You must brook them no quarter."

Baby suddenly felt very tired.

She put her hands in her lap. She closed her eyes and saw the shooting stars from her dream. She remembered the words that had accompanied the stars. "Necessary journey," whispered Baby.

"Write it down," said Eugenia. "Write down *mousetraps*."

Baby sighed. She opened her eyes and picked up her pencil and wrote down the word *mouse*.

Eugenia looked over her shoulder. "You have not written the complete word," she said. "The complete word is *mousetraps.*"

From far away came the sound of a train whistle.

Eugenia tapped her finger on the table. "What are you waiting for, Baby? Write *traps.*"

The train whistle sounded again, closer this time.

"No," said Baby. She laid down the pencil.

"I beg your pardon?" said Eugenia.

"No," said Baby. "I will not write the word *traps.*" She pushed the paper away from her. She stood. She said, "Sister, I am going on a trip."

"Yes," said Eugenia. "You are. You are going to Clyde's Bait, Feed, Tackle, and Animal Necessities, and once you are there you will purchase mousetraps."

"No," said Baby. "I am going on a different kind of trip."

"A different kind of trip?" said Eugenia.

Baby closed her eyes, and again she saw the shooting stars. "I am going on a necessary journey."

"I don't know what you're talking about," said Eugenia.

Baby opened her eyes. She didn't know exactly what she was talking about either. But she knew that something important was happening. Her heart was beating very fast.

The sun was shining into the kitchen, and everything seemed outlined in brightness, possibility.

Eugenia stared at Baby. Her mouth was open. She looked quite astonished.

Baby was astonished, too.

She carefully pushed her chair under the table. She smoothed the front of her skirt. "Now," she said, "if you will excuse me, Sister, I must go and pack for my journey."

Chapter Two

Baby went into her bedroom and closed the door.

"What next?" she said out loud.

Well, the obvious thing was that she must pack a suitcase. That was what people did when they went on journeys.

Baby retrieved her suitcase from the top shelf of her closet and opened it. Several surprised and hopeful moths flew out of the emptiness.

Baby looked down at the open suitcase.
She wasn't certain what to put in it.

She had no idea where she was going or
how long she would be gone. Also, the last
time she had packed a suitcase, Eugenia
had been standing right next to her, telling
her exactly what she must do and exactly
how she must do it.

Baby thought for a while.

"A toothbrush," she said out loud. "I will definitely need a toothbrush."

She put her toothbrush in the suitcase. It looked lonely. She added a nightgown and reading glasses.

The reading glasses made Baby realize that she should bring along something to read.

She put her current library book into the suitcase. The book was a mystery entitled *The Inimitable Spigot*. Detective Henrik Spigot was a man with a mustache who was always telling other people what they should do and how they should do it. He was very judgmental. He was extremely certain.

Baby thought that Detective Spigot bore a strong resemblance to Eugenia. Except for the mustache, of course.

Baby was on page 23 of the book and so far she didn't think that Spigot was particularly inimitable.

She looked down at the book and her toothbrush and her nightgown. She added a sweater to the suitcase and then she closed the lid and snapped the buckles shut. The buckles were made of brass, and they made a lovely, definitive, necessary-journey kind of sound.

There was a knock at the door.

"Baby?" said Eugenia.

Baby opened the door. "Yes, Sister?" she said.

"I would like to ask you some questions about your journey," said Eugenia.

"All right," said Baby.

"Where are you going?" said Eugenia.

"I'm not certain," said Baby.

"*Why* are you going?" said Eugenia.

"I cannot say," said Baby.

"Stop this nonsense," said Eugenia.

"I will not stop," said Baby. She picked up her suitcase.

General Washington, who was Eugenia's cat, came slinking around the corner. He twined himself through Baby's legs so aggressively that she felt as if she might lose her balance.

"Moooowwwwwwwwwlllllllll," said General Washington.

"General Washington is asking you not to go," said Eugenia in a somewhat subdued tone. "He is saying that he would like you to stay."

"What about you, Sister?" said Baby. "Would you like me to stay?" Baby knew, suddenly, that if Eugenia said the right words, she might put down her suitcase. She might stay.

15

Eugenia cleared her throat. She made a *harrump*-ish sort of noise. And then she straightened her shoulders.

"Far be it from me to tell you what to do," said Eugenia.

These were not the right words.

Baby tightened her grip on her suitcase. "If you will excuse me, Sister, I must leave now," said Baby. "It is necessary." She walked past Eugenia and General Washington.

Baby walked out the front door and down the front path and onto Deckawoo Drive. She took a right.

The suitcase was not heavy at all.

The sun was shining, and Baby's heart felt like a hummingbird in her chest. It was whirring. She could feel the flutter of its tiny wings.

She walked quickly. She did not look behind her. She was worried that Eugenia might be following her.

She was also a tiny bit hopeful that Eugenia might be following her.

When Baby was almost at the end of the block, she heard someone call her name.

"Baby! Baby Lincoln, wait for me!"

Baby stopped. She turned around.

Stella, who lived next door to the Lincolns, was running toward her.

"Where are you going, Baby Lincoln?" said Stella.

Baby stood up straighter. She said, "Hello, Stella. I am going on a necessary journey."

Chapter Three

"Oh," said Stella, "I like journeys. I have taken lots of journeys, but I'm not sure I've ever been on a *necessary* journey. Most of my journeys have been family journeys, and that means we all go together in the car and my mother drives, and my father sleeps, and Frank navigates. When we are on family journeys, we eat in restaurants, and I always order a hot dog and Frank doesn't order anything at all because he brings a supply of peanut butter sandwiches with him. He says that the peanut butter sandwich is infallible. Do you like peanut butter, Baby Lincoln?"

"I do like peanut butter," said Baby.

She felt a little niggle of worry. She realized that she had not packed anything to eat. She moved her suitcase from one hand to the other. She felt *The Inimitable Spigot* slide around in the near emptiness.

"The thing about our journeys," said Stella, "is that Frank is always the navigator. Always. I would like to hold the map sometimes. I would like to navigate. But I never get to."

"I understand," said Baby. "Eugenia will never allow me to hold the map either."

"Do you have a map?" said Stella. "We could look at it together."

"I do not have a map," said Baby. She felt another ping of worry.

"Well, where are you going?" said Stella.

"Right now?" said Baby.

"Right now," said Stella.

"I am headed to the train station," said Baby.

"I will walk with you," said Stella. She put her hand in Baby's hand. "Okay?"

"That would be lovely," said Baby.

▶ ▶ ▶

At the train station, the ticket seller said, "Headed where?"

Stella said, "Her name is Baby Lincoln, and she is on a necessary journey."

"Uh-huh," said the ticket seller. "Headed where?"

"I'm not entirely certain," said Baby.

The ticket seller was holding a cheese sandwich in both hands. His name tag said LAWRENCE.

Lawrence looked at Baby. He looked at Stella. He sighed. He put the sandwich down on the counter. The cheese inside the sandwich was orange and there were several thick slices of it. It looked delicious. Baby wished that she had thought to make herself a cheese sandwich before leaving home.

Lawrence reached out and picked up a leaflet from the display in front of him.

"Schedule," he said, handing it to Baby. "Pick a destination."

"Thank you very much," said Baby.

"Let me see, let me see," said Stella.

They stepped away from the ticket counter and Baby handed Stella the schedule.

"Ohhhh," said Stella. "It's a chart. I'm really good with math and charts. Last year, Mrs. Wilkinson said that I was a true math whiz. Has anybody ever called you a true math whiz, Baby Lincoln?"

"Not that I can recall," said Baby.

Eugenia was the sister who had a head for figures. Or at least that was what Eugenia said.

Stella studied the schedule. "How much money do you have, Baby Lincoln? You can go to Calaband Darsh if you have enough money. Doesn't Calaband Darsh sound like a good place to go?"

Calaband Darsh sounded like a very grand place, a shooting-star kind of place. Baby opened her purse and took out her wallet. She handed the wallet to Stella and watched as Stella counted the money inside.

"Okay," said Stella. She handed the wallet back to Baby. She consulted the train schedule. "Let's see."

It turned out that Baby didn't have enough money to get to Calaband Darsh.

She had enough money to get to Fluxom.

"Fluxom?" said Baby.

"Fluxom," said Stella.

Fluxom did not sound like a shooting-star kind of place at all.

But Baby went bravely back to the ticket counter and spoke to Lawrence. She said, "One ticket for Fluxom, please."

And after that, there was no turning back.

Baby boarded the train. Stella stood on the platform and waved good-bye.

The train lurched forward. Baby watched Stella get smaller and smaller until, finally, she disappeared altogether.

And then Baby Lincoln was alone, on a train, on a necessary journey.

Chapter Four

"Seat taken?" said a man wearing a gigantic fur hat.

The hat was so enormous and so furry that at first glance, Baby mistook the man for a bear.

"It is not taken," said Baby.

"Thank you very much," said the man. He sat down next to Baby. "Head allergies," he said. He pointed at his fur hat with an index finger. "I beg your pardon, but the hat must remain."

"Certainly," said Baby.

The man in the fur hat got out a newspaper. He skipped over the news and the sports and the opinions and went directly to the comics.

Eugenia said that the comics were a spectacular waste of time. Each morning, she removed them from the paper as a protest against their pointlessness.

The man in the fur hat followed each word of the comics with one enormous finger. He laughed softly as he read.

"Good for the head allergies," the man said to Baby when he saw her staring at him.

"I beg your pardon?" said Baby.

"Laughing," said the man. "Clears the sinuses and the soul in a very satisfying way."

"I see," said Baby. "Thank you."

The man rustled the pages of the paper. He laughed some more. And then he folded the paper carefully and took out a handkerchief and blew his nose for what seemed like a very long time.

He turned to Baby. "Did you bring something to read?"

"I brought my library book," said Baby. "It is a mystery entitled *The Inimitable Spigot.*"

"Is it funny?" said the man.

"It is not," said Baby. "My sister, Eugenia, recommended it to me."

"Would you care for a page of the comics?" said the man.

"Eugenia says that the comics are a spectacular waste of time."

The man in the fur hat laughed very loudly. "Why, of course they are." He slapped his knee. He laughed some more. "A spectacular waste of time! Absolutely! Yes. That is exactly what they are, bless them." He sneezed. He took out his handkerchief and blew his nose. He chuckled.

And then he turned to Baby with a very serious look on his face. "You must read the comics," he said. "I insist." The man unfolded the paper and handed Baby a page of the comics.

To be polite, Baby took the page. She held it out in front of her and placed a finger under each word in the first comic, just as she had seen the man in the fur hat do.

She glanced over at him.

"That's right," he said. "Keep going."

Baby looked at the pictures and read the words. In the first strip, there was a little man who had antennae on his head and who spoke in a strange language that resembled English just enough that Baby could make some sense of it. "Fozwhat mortak, I greet you!" said the man with the antennae. The picture showed him bending over, smiling at a bug on the sidewalk.

Baby read this and laughed. "Fozwhat mortak!" she said out loud.

"Yes!" said the man in the fur hat.

Baby went on to the next comic, which featured a squirrel that was able to fly and that was engaged in fighting evil. This strip was not quite as funny, but it was deeply satisfying in some ridiculous way. A squirrel! Fighting evil! Baby smiled to herself as she read it.

"You see?" said the man in the fur hat.

"I do!" said Baby.

Baby read the comics. She laughed. The man in the fur hat sat beside her, blowing his nose, nodding and smiling. Outside the train window, the world rushed by in a blur of green and gold and brown.

And Baby was suddenly tremendously
happy, just as she had been in her dream.

"Lower Loring!" shouted the conductor. "Lower Loring."

"This is my stop," said the man in the fur hat. He stood. He lifted the hat off his head and bowed to Baby. "It has been a pleasure, a delight, a revelation. It has been everything except a spectacular waste of time. Fozwhat mortak! I bid you safe travels. Tell your sister, Eugenia, that I send her greetings. Tell her to laugh."

Baby doubted that she would deliver this message to Eugenia, but she did think that she might start reading the comics on a regular basis.

"Good-bye," said Baby. "And thank you."

The man put the fur hat back on his head and lumbered down the aisle.

He really did look very much like a bear.

Baby heard him sneeze before he exited the train.

Chapter Five

Baby opened her suitcase and took out *The Inimitable Spigot.* She tried to read, but the book was not funny. Also, Henrik Spigot was annoying, and bossy. He thought he knew the answer to everything.

Baby closed the book and looked at the picture of Detective Spigot on the cover.

"No one knows the answer to everything," Baby said to Detective Spigot.

He really did look a lot like Eugenia — minus the mustache, of course.

Baby wondered what Eugenia was doing. Was she at Clyde's Bait, Feed, Tackle, and Animal Necessities? Was she purchasing mousetraps?

Did she miss Baby?

In answer to this last question, Baby heard Eugenia say, "Most certainly not!"

It was a very sad answer, even if it was an imaginary one.

Baby closed her eyes. She fell asleep.

When she woke up, a young woman was sitting beside her. The woman had long blond hair. There was a gigantic bag of jelly beans in her lap.

"Hi," said the woman. She smiled. "You were talking in your sleep. Something about mousetraps. I'm Sheila Marsden."

"I am Baby Lincoln," said Baby. "How do you do?"

"Baby?" said Sheila.

"Baby," said Baby.

"Your parents named you *Baby*?"

"No," said Baby. "That is what my sister, Eugenia, named me. Very early on, Eugenia said, 'I don't care what her name is. I am going to call her Baby. She is the baby, my baby.' And so I became Baby. And remained Baby."

"Wow," said Sheila. "That's kind of intense. What's your real name?"

"Lucille Abigail Eleanor Lincoln," said Baby. It felt strange to say her real name.

Sometimes Baby even forgot she had one.

"Lucille Abigail Eleanor Lincoln," repeated Sheila. "Cool. I like that name. Do you want a jelly bean, Lucille?"

Sheila held out the bag of jelly beans. Baby selected a yellow one. "Eugenia often says that jelly beans are bad for the teeth," said Baby. She put the jelly bean in her mouth. It tasted like sunshine. "Eugenia is not a fan of the jelly bean."

"That doesn't surprise me," said Sheila. "Have another one." She held out the bag again.

Baby selected a green jelly bean. It tasted like green leaves, things growing, springtime. She closed her eyes and chewed. The jelly bean was wonderful.

"So, where are you headed, Lucille?"

Lucille? Who was Lucille? And then Baby remembered. *She* was Lucille.

"I don't know where I'm headed," said Baby. "Well, I do know. I'm going to Fluxom. But it is more complicated than that. You see, I am on a necessary journey."

"That's cool," said Sheila. "Necessary journeys are cool. I'm on my way back to college, which is necessary, I guess." She shook the jelly bean bag. "Have another one," she said.

Baby selected a white jelly bean. She wondered if it would taste like snow.

"You can take more than one at a time, you know," said Sheila. "You can take a whole handful if you want to."

Baby leaned in closer to Sheila. She considered the bag. She took a purple jelly bean and a white one with yellow spots and several more green ones. She put them all in her mouth at once and chewed. Baby hadn't realized how hungry she was. She was glad that Sheila Marsden and her jelly bean bag had shown up.

Baby leaned back in her seat. The train seemed to be going faster, and from somewhere far away Baby heard music. It was a song that she knew but couldn't quite place.

"Do you hear music?" she said to Sheila.

"I hear something," said Sheila. She closed her eyes. She was quiet. "I've got a physics professor who says that the stars sing to each other all the time. Isn't that cool? Maybe the music we're hearing is the stars singing."

Did the stars really sing? Why had no one told Baby that before?

"Have another jelly bean, Lucille," said Sheila.

Baby leaned forward to inspect the jelly beans. Sunlight streamed in through the train window. Dust motes danced in the beams of light. Baby could still hear the music playing somewhere very far away. She felt another wave of happiness wash over her.

"Take a handful," said Sheila.

Baby took a handful.

Chapter Six

Sheila got off the train at Hickam Briar. She stood on the platform and waved to Baby. She called out, "Good-bye, Lucille! Good-bye!"

Sheila left Baby with an assortment of jelly beans tied up in a handkerchief. The handkerchief had Sheila's initials embroidered on it.

"See?" said Sheila when she gave Baby the handkerchief. "S.A.M. Those are my initials. Sheila Ann Marsden. My father embroidered that. He is very good with a needle and thread. If he knew you, he would sew your initials onto a handkerchief, too. Lucille Abigail Eleanor Lincoln. L.A.E.L."

Baby thought that she would miss Sheila quite a bit, but she didn't have time to miss her, because soon after the Hickam Briar station, the conductor appeared in the aisle by Baby's seat. With the conductor was a very small boy with a paper crown on his head and a sign around his neck. The sign said TRAVELING ALONE. PLEASE TREAT WITH EXTREME CARE, GENTLENESS, AND ALSO SOME CAUTION. HEADED TO FLATIRON IN CARE OF HIS AUNT GERTRUDE.

"My goodness," said Baby.

"I was wondering if you could keep an eye on this boy," said the conductor. "I was wondering if you could, uh, protect him."

The boy looked deeply unhappy. His eyes were red. His crown was crooked.

"Me?" said Baby.

No one had ever asked her to protect anyone.

"Yes," said the conductor. "You."

"Of course," said Baby. "I would be delighted."

"Good," said the conductor. "As the sign says, the boy is traveling alone."

The conductor cleared his throat. "And he is worried that, uh, wolves might attack the train."

"Wolves?" said Baby.

"That is his concern," said the conductor. "He has expressed it to me several
times in a very, uh, vehement fashion.
Wolves. Attacking the train."

The boy crossed his arms over his sign.
He looked down at the floor. He was really
very small to be traveling alone.

"You sit here," said the conductor to
the boy, "in the aisle seat, see? And if the
wolves come in through the window like
you say they will, then they will, uh, get
to this lady first, and that will slow them
down some, right? Okay?"

"My goodness," said Baby. An image of
the wolf from "Little Red Riding Hood"
popped into her head. His teeth gleamed
in a menacing way. Baby shook her head to
dispel the wolf. She patted the seat beside

her and smiled at the boy. "Sit down," she said.

The boy sat down and the conductor heaved a dramatic sigh. "Right," he said. "Good luck to both of you."

The conductor walked away, and the boy sat staring straight ahead with his arms still crossed over his sign.

"Well," said Baby. "Here we are."

"I'm not supposed to talk to strangers," said the boy.

"Of course," said Baby. "I understand." She got out Sheila's handkerchief and untied the knot. "Would you care for a jelly bean?" she said.

"I'm not supposed to take candy from strangers," said the boy.

"But I've been assigned to protect you," said Baby.

The boy looked up at Baby. His eyes were a bright blue. He looked down at the jelly beans.

It became very quiet on the train.

The boy sighed. He said, "Wolves have very sharp teeth."

Baby nodded.

"And when wolves get hungry, they do terrible things," said the boy. "Like attack trains."

Baby nodded again. "I believe you," she said. "Have a jelly bean."

The boy leaned forward. He unfolded his arms. He selected a yellow jelly bean.

"My name is George," he said.

Baby felt a small shiver of happiness.

"George is a wonderful name," said
Baby. "I am glad to meet you, George.
My name is Lucille."

And saying her name, her real name,
caused Baby to feel another ripple of joy.

Chapter Seven

George said, "I thought that this yellow jelly bean would taste like lemon, but it tastes like pear."

"Do you like it?" said Baby.

George nodded. "I like pears. My aunt Gertrude has lots and lots of pear trees in her backyard. She probably has a hundred pear trees. I am going to stay with my aunt Gertrude. But I only agreed to go because of the pears."

Baby nodded.

"Something terrible has happened," said George.

"Oh, dear," said Baby.

"Something horrible," said George.

"Does it have to do with wolves?" said Baby.

And then, to Baby's horror and dismay, George started to cry.

It was a crisis. And Eugenia was the sister who was good in a crisis, not Baby.

"Oh, no," said Baby. "Oh, dear." She emptied the jelly beans onto her lap and handed Sheila Marsden's monogrammed handkerchief to George. Her hands were shaking.

"I am so afraid," said George. He clutched the handkerchief. He cried louder.

Baby understood being afraid. When she was young, she had been afraid of every-thing: bats, bicycles, dusk, the darkness that followed dusk. Doorbells. She had, for some reason, been absolutely terrified of doorbells. Being alone had frightened her. And so had Mondays.

Eugenia was afraid of nothing, of course.

But whenever Baby had been afraid, Eugenia would sit with her in the green chair in the living room and read aloud to her. There was a lamp next to the green chair and the lamp made a yellow pool of light, and inside that pool of light, sitting next to Eugenia, Baby had been safe.

Baby felt a sudden, sharp pain high up in her chest.

She missed Eugenia.

George hiccupped. He used Sheila's handkerchief to blow his nose. "This handkerchief smells like jelly beans," he said. He took a deep breath and started to cry again.

"When I was a girl, I was frightened all the time," said Baby. "And when I was particularly frightened, my older sister would read to me, and that always made me feel safe. Would you like to hear a story?"

George nodded. "Yes," he said.

But then Baby remembered that the only book she had was *The Inimitable Spigot*. Her heart fell. She did not think that *The Inimitable Spigot* was the kind of book that would cheer anybody up. But she supposed it would have to do.

Baby opened the book. "Page One, Chapter One," said Baby.

George snuffled.

"'Detective Henrik Spigot was an extraordinary man, and was recognized by the department of police, the town of Winsome, and the whole of humanity as such. No mystery was truly a mystery to Detective Spigot—or at least it did not remain a mystery for long.

"'Detective Spigot lived alone in a green house on a high hill, and from there he could see the whole of Winsome spread out below him. The detective watched the people of the town from up high on his hill. He waited.'"

Baby paused.

George blew his nose into the handkerchief.

Detective Spigot is smug, Baby thought. *I do not care for him.*

George took a great gulp of air and held it in and then let it go in a *whoosh.*

"Aren't you going to read?" he said.

"Yes," said Baby. "But I was reading the wrong story."

"It wasn't much good," said George.

"I know," said Baby. "I will read the right story now."

"Good," said George.

Baby cleared her throat. She flipped to the middle of the book. She held *The Inimitable Spigot* up in front of her. "Chapter One," she said. "Once upon a time, there was a king. The king was wise and good. But he was lonely. And sometimes, late at night, he would stand in his garden and watch as stars fell through the night sky, chasing each other. The king was certain that he could hear music, the sound of the stars calling out to each other in the darkness. The music comforted the king."

Baby paused. The words she was reading weren't on the page at all. She, Lucille Abigail Eleanor Lincoln, was making them up.

"Keep going," said George.
And Baby did.

Chapter Eight

"The king had not always been a king. Once, he had been a boy who lived with his aunt in a small house on the side of a long, dark road. And behind this house, there grew pear trees, hundreds of them.

"The pear trees had been planted by a wizard named Calaband Darsh. And at the same time that the wizard planted the pear trees, he also cast a spell so that the boy, when he looked upon a pear, was able to see the entire universe hidden there. And this, it turned out, was a very good thing for a king to be able to do."

Baby felt George leaning in toward her.

She turned the page. "But I am getting ahead of myself. This is a long story," she read. Or pretended to read. "And it must be told right. All stories involving kings and wizards and wolves are important and must be told in a certain way and in their own time."

"There are wolves in this story?" said George.

"Of course," said Baby.

"Good," said George. "Keep going."

Baby read on.

The words of the story came to her without her thinking too much about what they should be. It was as if she were reading a book that already existed, telling a story that she already knew.

As she read, George leaned in closer and closer until, finally, he was leaning right up against her. He was warm. He smelled like peanut butter and construction paper.

"The wolves obeyed no man, of course," said Baby. "But they would sit and listen to the king. He could make it so that his human words made sense to their wolf ears and wolf hearts."

Baby looked down at George.

"Should I keep reading?" she said.

"Keep reading," said George.

It was late afternoon and the train was making a clickety-clackety sound as it headed through the universe.

Baby kept reading.

George's aunt Gertrude was waiting for him on the platform in Flatiron.

"That's her," said George. "There she is." He pointed.

Aunt Gertrude looked worried and flustered. She looked kind.

Baby's heart gave a small ping. Who would be waiting for her on the platform in Fluxom?

Eugenia would not be standing there. Eugenia was surely very, very angry at Baby for running away.

Eugenia was terrifying when she was angry. Baby's heart gave another, different kind of ping.

"Good-bye," said George.

He stood. He adjusted his crown. "Thank you for reading me the story. I could tell that you were making it up."

"You could?" said Baby.

George nodded. "I'm small," he said. "But I can read."

"Oh," said Baby. She was strangely disappointed.

"I need to know what happened to the king," said George.

"Well," said Baby. She felt a flush of happiness, certainty. "I will write to you. I will tell you what happens next."

"All of it?" said George. "The whole story?"

"Every bit of it," said Baby.

The conductor came to escort George off the train. Baby lowered the window. She shouted out to Aunt Gertrude. She said, "Hello, I am a friend of George and my name is Lucille Lincoln. I live at

Fifty-two Deckawoo Drive in Gizzford. If you write to me, I will write to George."

Aunt Gertrude smiled. She waved. She said, "Lucille at Fifty-two Deckawoo Drive! We will write to you!"

And then George was on the platform.
Aunt Gertrude hugged him. She enveloped
him.

The train started to move.

Aunt Gertrude and George waved at Baby, and Baby waved back.

"Good-bye, Lucille," shouted George.

His golden paper crown glinted in the last of the evening light.

Baby leaned back in her seat and closed her eyes. She thought about the house on Deckawoo Drive and the way the sun shone on the kitchen table in the early morning and again, from a different angle, in the late afternoon.

She thought about Eugenia sitting at the table.

Baby's heart clenched.

She wanted to go home.

Chapter Nine

It was dark in Fluxom.

The station platform was empty.

"Fluxom!" shouted the conductor. "Disembark for Fluxom!"

Baby took hold of her suitcase. She stood. The conductor helped her down the metal stairs.

And then the train pulled away and Baby was alone on the platform.

Somewhere, hidden in some scraggly bush by the train tracks, a cricket sang. The song was high and sweet and it made Baby feel even more lonely. She thought about the stars and how they sang to each other. She listened very closely, but she could not hear their music. She could only hear the lone cricket.

"Baby!" someone shouted.

Baby saw Eugenia and Stella walking toward her. Her heart thumped once, twice, three times. First it thumped in disbelief (Eugenia had come) and then it thumped in gratitude (Eugenia had come for her) and then, finally, it thumped with joy (Eugenia had come for Baby!).

"Baby Lincoln!" called Stella. "We came to meet your train! I knew where you were going and what time you would arrive because I was the one who read the train schedule. And I thought it would be very bad if you got off the train and no one was here to meet you. Wouldn't that have been very bad? And so Mr. Watson and Eugenia Lincoln and Mercy Watson and me drove all the way here. I navigated! I held the map! And Eugenia Lincoln was upset because she did not get to hold the map. And she was also upset because Mercy got to sit in the front seat. Mr. Watson and Mercy are waiting in the car, and you can hold the map on the way home if you want to, Baby Lincoln."

"This is all just ridiculous," said Eugenia. "It is absurd! I can't believe we drove with a pig in the front seat to the middle of nowhere."

"Oh, Sister," said Baby. "I missed you so."

Eugenia sniffed. She looked away.

"Eugenia missed you back!" said Stella. She jumped up and down. "She missed you and missed you and missed you. It's true. It's all she could talk about. 'Where is Baby? We must find Baby! What will I ever do without Baby? I would be lost without Baby.' That is what Eugenia said."

"Is that true, Sister?" said Baby. "Would you be lost without me?"

"Perhaps," said Eugenia. She stared off at the horizon.

"Tell her," said Stella. She took hold of Eugenia's hand and swung it back and forth.

"I missed you," whispered Eugenia. "I would be lost without you, Baby."

"Oh, Sister," said Baby.

"See?" said Stella. "*See?* You are two sisters who love each other. But we have to go now because Mr. Watson and Mercy are in the car and Mercy is hungry and the engine is running and it is a long drive. We have to go home. Let's go home."

"Let's," said Baby.

"Let's," said Eugenia. She picked up Baby's suitcase.

"Oh, Sister," said Baby. "I have so much to tell you."

Eugenia took hold of Baby's right hand. She said, "Well, if you insist on telling a story, I suppose I will have to listen."

Stella took hold of Baby's left hand. "We can talk and talk and talk," said Stella. "And when we get home, it will be almost morning and maybe Mrs. Watson will make us some toast with a great deal of butter on it."

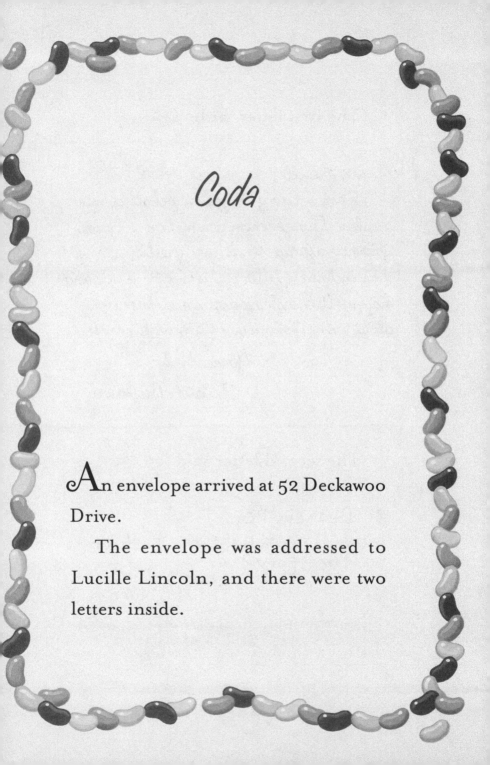

Coda

An envelope arrived at 52 Deckawoo Drive.

The envelope was addressed to Lucille Lincoln, and there were two letters inside.

The first letter said:

Dear Lucille,

I am writing to you on behalf of my nephew George whom you met on a train journey. George sends you greetings and has enclosed a letter of his own. He is well and happy. Although he does sometimes worry about wolves. Thank you for your kindness.

Yours truly,
Gertrude Nissbaum

The second letter said:

Dear Lucille,
Will you tell me the rest of the story?
Love, George

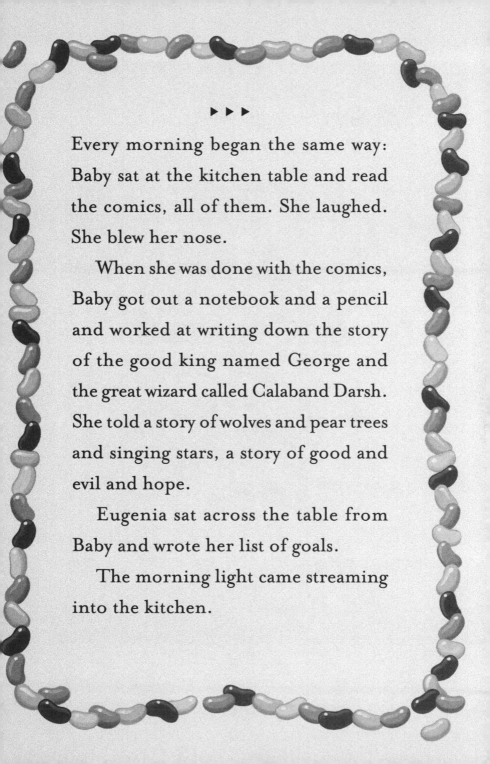

▶ ▶ ▶

Every morning began the same way:
Baby sat at the kitchen table and read
the comics, all of them. She laughed.
She blew her nose.

When she was done with the comics,
Baby got out a notebook and a pencil
and worked at writing down the story
of the good king named George and
the great wizard called Calaband Darsh.
She told a story of wolves and pear trees
and singing stars, a story of good and
evil and hope.

Eugenia sat across the table from
Baby and wrote her list of goals.

The morning light came streaming
into the kitchen.

Baby wrote her story.

She ate jelly beans as she worked.

The
Necessary
Journey

- by -
Lucille Abigail
Eleanor Lincoln

Kate DiCamillo is the renowned author of numerous books for young readers, including two Newbery Medal winners, *Flora & Ulysses* and *The Tale of Despereaux,* as well as the Mercy Watson and Tales from Deckawoo Drive series. She says, "When I set out on this journey with Baby, I had no idea what was going to happen. I only knew that the journey was necessary. And now that the journey is over, I have to say that I miss everyone I met along the way. I will miss George most of all. Maybe he will show up in another story? I will have to ask Baby about that."

Chris Van Dusen is the author-illustrator of *The Circus Ship, King Hugo's Huge Ego, Randy Riley's Really Big Hit,* and *Hattie & Hudson,* and the illustrator of the Mercy Watson and Tales from Deckawoo Drive series. He says, "Poor Baby Lincoln, always cowering in her big sister's shadow. It's refreshing to see her step out and have her own adventure for a change. But I have to admit, I can't get through this story without tearing up. Kate's words get me every time." Chris Van Dusen lives in Maine.

Navigate a neighborhood full of mishaps, mayhem, and a lot of hot buttered toast.

Tales from Deckawoo Drive

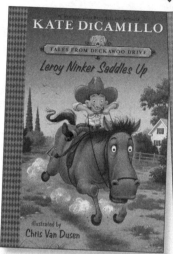

The original pig tales!

Featuring Chris Van Dusen's art in full color!